Can you be our donkey?

An Ivy and Mack s

Contents

Written by Juliet Clare Bell

Illustrated by Gustavo Mazali

with Tamara Joubert

Collins

What's in this story?

Listen and say

stage

theatre

Grandpa's band

Ivy and Mack were at Grandpa's house. He played his guitar for them. "These songs are for a **show** at the theatre. I'm playing there with my band."

"What's the show about, Grandpa?" asked Mack.

"It's called *Please Come Home*. It's about a donkey that loves dancing."

"A dancing donkey!" Ivy and Mack laughed.

"How does it dance?" asked Mack.

"Like this!" said Grandpa. He showed them the donkey's dance.

Ivy and Mack **practised** the dance. It was very funny.

Ivy wanted to see *Please Come Home*, on her birthday.

"Can we go to the theatre, Dad," asked Ivy. "P-L-E-A-S-E!"

Mack pointed at the computer. "Can you look on the computer, Dad?"

"OK," said Dad. "There are four tickets on your birthday, Ivy."

Chapter 2 This is fantastic!

On Saturday, it was Ivy's birthday. At 5 o'clock it was time to go to the theatre. Ivy was very **excited**.

When they got to the theatre, Ivy and Mack stood with their mouths open.

"The theatre is beautiful!" said Mack.

Everyone sat down and waited. Then the music started and everyone was quiet.

"It's Grandpa! I can see him … and I can see Grandpa's band," said Mack.

Ivy looked at Mack. "*Sssshhh!*"

Ivy watched the family and their donkey on the stage. The donkey was blue and it was very sad.

The donkey wanted to dance but the children laughed at it. It was very sad and it ran away.

When it was time for a **break**, the music stopped and everyone clapped. The **theatre curtain** came down in front of the stage.

"Would you like an ice cream, *birthday girl*?" asked Mum. The show starts again in 20 **minutes**."

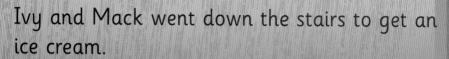

Ivy and Mack went down the stairs to get an ice cream.

"I can't choose," said Ivy.

"I want them *all!*" said Mack.

Chapter 3 Something's wrong

When they got to the front of the line, Ivy saw Grandpa. He didn't look happy.

"Why aren't you with your band?" asked Ivy.

"I wanted to find you!" said Grandpa.

"There were two children **inside** the donkey," said Grandpa. "They fell and hurt their legs. They can't be the donkey now."

"Oh dear! What does that mean?" asked Ivy.

"We haven't got a donkey now," said Grandpa.

"But you *need* the donkey for the dancing!" said Ivy.

Grandpa looked at Ivy and Mack. "I know," he said. "Can *you* be our donkey?"

"But we don't know what to do!" said Mack.

Grandpa smiled. "Yes, you do! You listened to the music at my house. And you learned the dance. Can you do the same thing again?"

Ivy was sad. She loved the play. "I want to *watch* the end of the show," she said. "We can't *watch* it when we're *in* it."

"No, ... but don't you want to go on the stage?" asked Mack.

"Well, ... it's fun when everyone claps!" said Ivy.

It's my Birth day!

19

Chapter 4 Ivy and Mack on stage

Ivy and Mack went behind the stage. Grandpa gave Ivy the donkey's head.

"You are the front of the donkey," said Grandpa.

"And I'm the back!" laughed Mack.

Ivy and Mack met Daisy. She had pink hair and a big smile. She helped Ivy and Mack get dressed for the show.

Ivy and Mack practised. They walked and danced inside the donkey.

"Fantastic!" said Daisy.

Ivy and Mack went on to the stage. When the donkey music started, Mack jumped.

"Quick!" said Ivy. "Let's move!"

The theatre curtain went up. The donkey's family came onto the stage. Mack and Ivy danced to the little girl.

"I think this is wrong, Mack!" said Ivy from inside the donkey. "Go to the mum!"

Ivy and Mack danced the other way.

Ivy and Mack remembered the dance well.
They had fun.

Chapter 5 A very happy birthday!

The show finished. Everyone clapped.
Then Daisy came onto the stage.

"Thank you very much to Ivy and Mack,"
she said. "You were fantastic!"

Ivy was hot. She started to walk off the stage. Daisy smiled. "Don't go," she said. "We need to do one more thing."

"Listen, Ivy!" said Mack. "They're playing a song for you!"

"Happy Birthday to you, Happy Birthday to you. Happy Birthday, dear Ivy, Happy Birthday to you." Everyone in the theatre sang *Happy Birthday* to Ivy.

"Thank you, donkey," said Ivy. "This is the best birthday!"

Mini-dictionary

Listen and read

break (noun) A **break** is a short period of time at the theatre, when the show stops and you can get up and walk around.

excited (adjective) Someone who is **excited** is very happy because something good is happening.

inside (preposition) Someone or something that is **inside** a place or thing is in it.

minute (noun) **Minutes** are used to measure time. There are 60 minutes in one hour.

practise (verb) If you **practise** something, you do it a lot so that you can do it better.

show (noun) A **show** is when some people play music, sing or act for other people.

theatre curtain (noun) The **theatre curtain** is a long heavy piece of material that hangs in front of the stage when nobody is on it.

1 Look and order the story

2 Listen and say

Collins

Published by Collins
An imprint of HarperCollins*Publishers*
Westerhill Road
Bishopbriggs
Glasgow
G64 2QT

HarperCollins*Publishers*
1st Floor, Watermarque Building
Ringsend Road
Dublin 4
Ireland

William Collins' dream of knowledge for all began with the publication of his first book in 1819.

A self-educated mill worker, he not only enriched millions of lives, but also founded a flourishing publishing house. Today, staying true to this spirit, Collins books are packed with inspiration, innovation and practical expertise. They place you at the centre of a world of possibility and give you exactly what you need to explore it.

© HarperCollins*Publishers* Limited 2020

10 9 8 7 6 5 4 3 2

ISBN 978-0-00-839736-4

Collins® and COBUILD® are registered trademarks of HarperCollins*Publishers* Limited

www.collins.co.uk/elt

British Library Cataloguing in Publication Data

A catalogue record for this publication is available from the British Library.

Author: Juliet Clare Bell
Lead illustrator: Gustavo Mazali (Beehive)
Copy illustrator: Tamara Joubert (Beehive)
Series editor: Rebecca Adlard
Publishing manager: Lisa Todd
Product managers: Jennifer Hall and Caroline Green
In-house editor: Alma Puts Keren
Project manager: Emily Hooton
Editor: Deborah Friedland
Proofreaders: Natalie Murray and Michael Lamb
Cover designer: Kevin Robbins
Typesetter: 2Hoots Publishing Services Ltd
Audio produced by id audio, London
Reading guide author: Julie Penn
Production controller: Rachel Weaver
Printed and bound by: GPS Group, Slovenia

MIX
Paper from
responsible sources
FSC
www.fsc.org
FSC™ C007454

This book is produced from independently certified FSC™ paper to ensure responsible forest management.

For more information visit: **www.harpercollins.co.uk/green**

Download the audio for this book and a reading guide for parents and teachers at www.collins.co.uk/839736